Winter's Curse

Mary Catelli

Published by Wizard's Wood Press, 2016.

WINTER'S CURSE

First edition. May 8, 2016.

Copyright © 2016 Mary Catelli.

Written by Mary Catelli.

Winter's Curse

The wind swirled about the firs, in streamers of snow. Snowflakes rose as much as they fell, and elsewhere drifted along on a level, as if sauntering by.

Gareth eyed the firs—they were only trees—and looked over his shoulder to the rest of the patrol. "Nothing more! We've got to get back! Our foes won't need to fear the storm!"

The bulky form that was the captain hesitated, and Gareth's parched lips set. He wondered how many men had made the appeal before; they all had faced the captain at his words, but their hoods shielded their expressions. The captain stood, pondering, as if there were any question whether their scouting would prove useful in this storm.

The captain's shoulders slumped. "Head back!"

Will marvels never cease? thought Gareth. He slogged back, his feet sinking up to his knees with every step, and snow slipping into the boot. When he reached the others, Brand looked at him. Snow clung to the fur lining his hood.

"If Zavrien has such fearful powers," said Gareth, sharply, "why doesn't he make himself somewhere *pleasant* to live?"

A gust shoved them forward. After a minute, Brand said, his voice dejected, flat, "He can't be that powerful. Not if he needs to protect himself from us."

Gareth grimaced. The wind stung his face with snow, and he lowered his head against it to trudge on. Amazing, how eager he could be for the shelter of a few tents and still fewer fires, kept alive only by endless magic.

His hood blocked off everything except the snow before him, where the footsteps, rough shapes from the beginning, were rapidly deformed by the wind. After plodding minutes, his foot slid on ice. He clambered back to his feet and looked about.

He could not pick out another soldier in the swirling snow, or any landmark. His own footsteps vanished as swiftly as falling snow and blowing wind could muffle them. Hollows in the snow ahead no longer looked like footprints, even vaguely.

"Brand!" he shouted. The wind snatched his words. "BRAND! CAPTAIN! RUFUS!"

A narrow hand closed on his arm with a grip like steel. Even through his thick coat, he felt each distinct icy finger. His mouth abruptly dry, he turned his head.

An angular woman of pure blue, her eyes indifferent and inhuman, looked at him. Her lighting-blue hair flew on the wind, with the skirt of her thin, sleeveless dress. Gareth tried to jerk back and did not move an inch. He reached for his spear. The frost fairy stabbed at his face with her free hand. Cold surged from her fingers. The spear fell from his numb hands, and he could not move.

The frost fairy smiled. Gareth, unable to shift his eyes, stared at her and waited for the end: she had doomed him the moment she laid her hand on him.

But the cold did not extend, did not reach his heart and be his death. Nor did her smile shift.

Another creature lumbered from the veil of snow. He caught glimpses of a paler blue before an enormous hand and arm, translucent white with blue deep inside, came through his vision and closed around his waist. The giant lifted Gareth, giving him a brief glimpse of eyebrows like snowdrifts and wrinkles like icicles before throwing him over his shoulder. Gareth, unable even to blink, stared at a back like ice on a cliff-face.

"Hurry," said the frost fairy, her voice crackling. "Zavrien will not be pleased with slowness."

The giant said nothing but trudged steadily into the wind, jolting Gareth with each step. The frost fairy danced about the giant, muttering about speed. Snow flew over the giant's shoulder into Gareth's face. He blinked, sputtering. The frost fairy's attack wore off, then. He wriggled. The giant's hand tightened, and Gareth subsided. For an alarming moment, he glanced at the frost fairy, dancing on the wind, but though she spied his movements with sharp glances, she did not lay a finger on him, or even approach closer.

As if she needed to. His toes felt like chunks of ice against his feet. Gareth closed his eyes, and time blurred. God have mercy on me, he thought, and could not manage any more thought. At least he did not feel as if he were no longer cold, which would be a sign of the end—and then the thought struck, colder than the frost fairy's fingers, that he should await that moment with eagerness, as the only end of this pain.

The giant's walk went on and on, jouncing Gareth. Now and again, he felt the giant going up a slope, or down one. Then, the wind cut off as if with a knife. For a moment, he wondered if he dreamed. The giant's footsteps crunched against the ice-covered snow for a minute more; then he lifted Gareth from his shoulder.

In a field of snow, a man in a black sorcerer's robe, embroidered with coppery runes, stood with his hands clasped behind his back. His pale features held no emotion. His black hair and beard showed not a trace of snow, and though his clothing was light, he did not shiver.

"So. A soldier of the army." His melodious voice held no more emotion than his face. "The oh-so-luminous force of righteousness and truth. Eager to hunt through the north lands for the evil sorcerers."

The army, Gareth thought, had not conjured snow storms and the deaths of hundreds, leaving skeletons—and skeletons of children—scattered through the snow.

His mouth felt too leaden to move.

He could not feel the giant's grip on his arms; Zavrien would not have him much longer. Out of the depths I cry to You, o Lord, he thought, but could recall no more.

"What, nothing to say?"

Gareth swayed.

Zavrien raised his hand. Violet flames leapt from it to Gareth. Heat stabbed through his body, restoring feeling, and pain. Gareth gasped.

"Escape is not that easy," said Zavrien. He looked at the frost fairy. "Go, watch the army."

Gareth looked away as the woman flitted into the blizzard, vanishing when she reached the snowfall.

"You do not like my servants?" said Zavrien. His face contorted. "They are faithful. They are loyal. They obey me. They do not appease you with words sweet as honey and brief as dew." Gareth wondered at the passion, but if that showed in his face, Zavrien paid no heed. The wizard's breath came rapidly. "As for you, soldier, here is what I give to an invader."

His finger touched Gareth's cheek and drew straight down it.

"Ill luck follow you all your days."

His finger jabbed in other lines.

"And all who fare with you. Let it blight you, day and night, until your death."

Gareth could see a bit of black against his cheeks. He closed his eyes. Winter's Curse—he knew the mark. He should have known when the frost fairy first laid a hand on him. Why else would Zavrien have him kept alive?

But Zavrien had already turned away, and said, carelessly, "Bring him back."

The giant nodded and threw Gareth to his shoulder. The cold returned, seeping back into his body. It would not kill him in time. Soon enough, but not in time.

Perriel tried to peer through the wind-driven snow, but though her wall of air protected her from the wind, the snow all but blinded her. Those dark shapes ahead might be firs.

She shivered. The stories were too feeble. She could not have imagined this storm. If apprentices were brought here, the warnings about diabolerie would be much sharper. It might even have dissuaded Master Rodger. . . .

"Perriel!" Corry's voice rang through the wind on the wings of his spell. "The general wants us back."

"They found the rest?"

"Some." Corry emerged from the whiteness, shaking his head. "We can't risk the searchers, too."

A strand of hair had worked its way out of her braid; it poked her face. Perriel shoved it back. "We haven't found half of them!"

Corry came within the ambit of her spell, and snow no longer blew between them. His puppy-dog eyes were sorrowful. "The general's going to break the captain."

"Maybe the captain should stay behind to search."

Corry did not answer. Then, he had learned to—humor her indignation. He seldom lifted a finger to actually help.

Perriel looked away, toward the firs. "I'll just check this grove."

Corry shrugged. "I'll come with you. Two can search twice as fast."

Which meant he thought that would indeed get them back to camp earlier.

Perriel trudged through the drifts. Snow clumped in every crease in her clothing.

Corry followed, more slowly. "If we had known we would be stuck with this, we might have been less eager to deal with our master."

"Just as well we didn't know, then, isn't it?" Perriel said, tartly. She had known that Corry had followed her lead, back then, but to wish that. . . .

She wondered if Zavrien had had an apprentice who had not been eager to deal with his master, who hesitated to denounce—well, she should not think ill of the dead, who were past any judgment of *hers*. Any such apprentice had paid a stern price for his reluctance—but, she thought with a touch of acid, he had not been the only one to pay.

The firs blocked some of the wind, and much of the blowing snow. The air was almost transparent, the drifts were smaller, and a brown lump, touched with white, lay at the grove's edge—like a soldier, overcome by cold.

Perriel hurried. Snow already gathered on him, filling folds in the cloth, but a man lay there. She held a hand to his lips, and a warm breath hit her fingers. Her own breath rushed out. He looked no older than she, or Corry, was, but he was solidly built. The two of them would be hard put to carry him along.

"Corry!" She put her arms around the unconscious man. He groaned. Fearing frost-bite, Perriel turned him over. His dark hair fell over his face—his very pale face—and she shoved it aside. His eyes were still closed. On one cheek rested a sigil, black and sharp as if painted with ink. Cold from more than the weather, Perriel recognized, though she could not read, the mark. Her hand went to his cheek, trying to rub it away. The soldier jerked, but the black did not diminish.

The chilly tent was lit, and warmed a little, only by a newly lit magefire. General Ryna Iceeyes slapped her gloves into her hand. Perriel felt small, negligible, and mute. Corry knelt, silent by the cot where the soldier—Gareth—lay.

"We should not have taken you. We were not that desperate for wizards," said General Ryna. "A veteran would not have been such a fool."

Gareth murmured in his fever.

"What would the veteran have done?" Perriel said. "Left him to freeze?"

"Yes," said Ryna. A startled noise spilled from Corry's mouth, and her lip curled. "And we thought you were hard because you denounced your own master."

"Abandoning him would be murder," said Perriel, her voice sounding light in her own ears.

"He has no right to bring his curse among us!" said the general. "A plague-bearer could be forbidden the camp, and this is worse than a plague!"

"And," said a captain, "it would have been kinder. Freezing to death is not that hard a way to die."

Perriel took a step backwards. Her voice grew plaintive. "Can't the curse be lifted? The Spell-Breaker...."

"No one has," said Ryna. The wind buffeted the tent. "No one under Winter's Curse has lived long enough for many attempts to be made."

Corry rose. His dark eyes were troubled. "If he is dangerous..."

"He's ill," Perriel said. Her gaze fell from Ryna's face, came back, and fell again. "The spells work quickly. If we cured him tonight and left him in the morning, he might—"

Ryna looked at her in cold silence.

"I'll stay the night with him," Perriel said.

"I could make you come away," said Ryna, softly.

"She's very hard to move once she's set on a path," said Corry.

Perriel opened her mouth to protest—she had never insisted on anything but reporting Master Rodger's diabolerie, which could have *killed* them—but Ryna shrugged, and she closed her mouth. Tending Gareth came first. She could quibble with Corry later.

"We have nothing against him, child," said the general. "I know that some have spoken of him as promising, and it is a misfortune to lose him. But we will. All that matters is how many he takes with him." She turned to Corry. "Come with me, Corry. I wish to speak with you."

The tent darkened; falling snow clumped on the canvas, and the night approached. At least the light spell's steady warmth had managed to accumulate, taking the edge from the chill. Perriel studied the sigil—no paint, but an illusion on top of the curse. It was always harder to break a spell under an illusion; the illusion affected not only the sight, but a wizard's ability to discern what manner of curse it hid. She had seen that before, but never so masterful a concealment.

She supposed that holding the lands bound in winter showed a little skill at wizardry.

When, in the darkness, Corry came with supper, she asked for her spell-books. He glanced, frightened, at Gareth, but returned with the books—shoving them into the tent even more quickly than he had the supper.

Gareth occasionally rambled, but his sleep calmed. Perriel sat with her chosen book propped up against her knees for long, fruitless hours, but finally slept. A thought dawned on her just as the blankets grew warm: that Zavrien had found Gareth argued that he knew where the army was.

Briefly, Perriel thought of rousing, and warning the army. She turned over. A bitter draft touched her neck, and she huddled into the blankets again. Ryna, being a general, probably had thought of it already. Further proof, in her eyes, that Perriel was unfit for the army—thinking a wizard new to war could lecture a veteran—and rousing her from sleep to do it, no doubt.

Perriel drifted off to a sleep.

Light suffused the tent through the canvas, as if it were midmorning rather than dawn. Silence pervaded the camp. The storm had died down, but this was more than the want of the wind's blast.

Perriel tasted something bitter in her mouth.

Gareth coughed.

Perriel, oblivious to the cold, threw back the blankets, scrambled to her sock-clad feet, and ran to the door. She could recognize landmarks from when they had first camped here, when the snow had first approached, but the sun, half way to zenith, shone on glittering snow. Wind had obliterated every trace of the camp, leaving not even any hollows in the flatness before her. Chill attacked her fingers and nose, but Perriel could not move away. She could not have slept this late. If nothing else, the noise of breaking camp would have woken her.

Gareth shifted behind her. She let in cold on her patient as well as herself—not a virtue in a nurse.

Perriel let the flap fall from her fingers, though she felt so stunned that even that motion was difficult. She wondered if she would have defended Gareth, had she known that they would desert her, as well. General Ryna had threatened to force her—and Corry had argued against it. Had he convinced them that she would prove dangerous? Her fingers twisted together. She had known him for many years, as a child, as a fellow apprentice; she could not swear that he would not have. He might even have known it when he brought her dinner.

"Lord, have mercy on us," she whispered. She drew a deep breath. "Christ, have mercy on us. Lord, have mercy on us. St. Michael, Archangel, defend us in battle. St. David, pray for us. St. Casper, pray for us. St. Melchior, pray for us. St. Balthazar, pray for us." She swallowed. The two of them camped alone in a wilderness of endless winter—of an evil wizard's endless, enchanted winter. "St. Jude, pray for us."

Gareth groaned, startling her. "Water," he begged, his eyes still closed.

Just as well she had not known, then, Perriel decided virtuously. She turned slowly from the door and trudged over to their supplies. More had been brought in over the night: bread, cheese, dried meat, even some dried fruit. It was the same dried, hard, and tasteless meals they had always eaten in Zavrien's lands, but it would take long for them to starve on this.

Perriel's eyebrows rose. General Ryna must have had a conscience about abandonment. She picked up the water bottle. Though not much of one.

She propped Gareth up and held the water to his mouth, holding her hand steady by main force until Gareth stopped drinking. He slumped against her arm; she had to fight to not let him drop but lower him gently. He looked pitifully young.

If he did not survive—she lacked the winter lore to survive in this wilderness. Carefully, she capped the bottle, trying to suppress her hands' trembling. General Ryna knew how little she knew about the land.

Feeling pitifully young, Perriel managed only to put the bottle back before she collapsed against her cot, burying her face against the blankets.

Gareth's throat burned—again? he thought, vaguely. The dead silence made him wonder what had happened to his ears. He opened his eyes a crack and saw only canvas, with the sunlight behind it.

A low song came from behind him: a woman singing children's rhymes under her breath. He could not be deaf then.

He rolled over. A woman stood over packs of supplies with her back to him, her straw blond hair falling down her back in two braids. Gareth wondered who she was and swallowed. Pain stabbed through his throat. "Water," he pled.

The song cut off. A second later, she bent over him, putting her arm around his shoulders. He tried to sit without her help, but even that effort made him realize his weakness. The woman, her face set, held the water to his mouth. Gareth gulped, and his throat eased. The woman tilted the bottle, and Gareth drank more carefully, for fear of spilling it. The woman's pale, heart-shaped face was still strange to him, though he vaguely remembered something about water. A second later, his swallow got him only half a mouthful; he had drained the bottle. The woman pulled it back and lowered him to the cot.

No shapes outside cast shadows on the canvas, and he could still hear nothing. "What happened to the army?"

"They left." Her blue eyes met his, glanced at his cheek for a second, and looked back.

He let out his breath. He had asked the wrong question. He should have asked why he yet received shelter, water, and nursing. The woman had supplies from the army. She had to know. Someone would have told her if nothing else.

"Who are you?" he said.

"A fool." Her mouth twitched. "My name is Perriel. I am also a wizard."

The room was tiny, with a single, round window, but the bed was her familiar bed, with the blue quilt that her mother had made for her. Perriel smiled. What a dream she had had.

The breeze carried the smell of baking bread. She would have it with honey this morning, before Master Rodger reviewed the light spell with her. She pushed back the blanket.

Cold washed in, and Perriel blinked at the tent. Her patient slept, across the tent. She dragged in a deep breath and nearly froze her lungs. She hugged the blankets over her, and tears streaked hotly across her face. What a dream she had had, indeed.

Swirls of snow, like infant ghosts, ran over the plain. Slate-gray clouds covered the sky. Perriel shivered in the wind but could not step inside. After a week in the tent, with Gareth asleep most of the time, the occasional effort of melting snow over the magefire did not exhaust her, she had few spells she could practice, and even the frozen waste had some allure.

Gareth was asleep and, she decided, well enough to leave for a time. Her heart lightened at the thought. She pulled her heavy coat over the lighter one she wore in the tent and laced it against the wind. With a final glance to be sure Gareth did not stir, Perriel pulled up her hood and set out into the cold. Her feet sank into the snow, but no higher than her ankles. She walked briskly, the wind at her back.

The clouds turned the daylight into a brilliant white glow, and left the snowdrifts almost shadowless, where snow hissed as it poured before the wind. Perriel's toes, fingers, and nose tingled with cold, but it was such a relief to walk. Every now and then, she glanced behind herself to pick out the tent, but she could not stop walking, though the tent was nothing more than a dot on the snow.

Firs appeared ahead of her. Perriel stepped without thinking and slid on a patch of ice, landing on her face. She scrambled up and tried to brush the snow off. Some fell back, but the glittering crystals stuck. Then, she had had her walk. She turned.

The wind struck her in the face. Perriel blinked. The snow suddenly no longer rose in little swirls but in eddies, growing larger even as she watched. She had never seen it rise so quickly before.

She could still see the tent. After a glance at the distance, she stopped to cast the shield of air. The chill leached heat from her body as she wove the spell, but the stillness as the spell went up felt like warmth in itself. She started back.

Gusts of wind shoved the shield, again and again. The tent grew larger, but no more distinct. The air behind the shield, though calm, was still cold and would leach warmth from her. Perriel's mouth set as pushing against the snow grew harder. A misplaced foot slid against ice, twisted, and threw her into a snow bank. Perriel floundered to her feet again and blinked. Snow clung to her eyelashes. Her feet felt like chunks of ice, and her fingers were numb. She pulled her fingers from her gloves' fingers and tucked them into her palms to warm them.

Snow swirled, hiding the tent. Her mouth set, she trudged onward, picking out the shape as it appeared between gusts but still walked when it was hidden.

A pale face, surrounded by silvery gray hair, appeared in the whiteness and smiled. Perriel blinked. The smile deepened. The woman behind it, dressed in a sky-blue gown and cloak, emerged from the snow. She twirled, the silvery fringe on her clothing flying, and stopped to hold out her hand to Perriel. The wind sank, and with it the snow, letting her see again. All about the plain, frost fairies danced over the drifts.

Perriel blinked again. Her legs and arms felt like lead.

The frost fairy's voice slid through the shield. "Come, dance. Warm yourself."

That made sense. Moving would warm her. She held out her hand, and the frost fairy took it. Perriel felt warmer and smiled. The other frost fairies, beaming, gathered around her. Perriel tossed her head. Her hood fell back. Her blond hair spilled out— almost as pale as the fairies', thought Perriel.

Gareth rolled over and pushed back the covers. The chilly air in the tent was more bracing than unpleasant. He looked about and realized the woman—Perriel—was gone. He felt a cold weight in his stomach. The curse might have struck her. It did not take long for it to act.

The wind was not loud, but vague noises came from outside, like footsteps on packed snow. For a moment, his heart seemed to stop. Then it hammered in his chest.

He forced himself to his feet—easier than he would have guessed—donned his boots, and went over to the door, grabbing his coat on the way. Pushing open the flap sent icy air, and a swirl of snowflakes, into his face. Perriel stood not five paces away, her blond hair bare. A frost fairy held the wizard's hand as she leached the warmth from Perriel's body. More than a dozen frost fairies gathered around. Their pale skirts of green, blue, and white swirled, and they smiled in wolfish anticipation.

His heart hammered. Once, he had seen a man who had danced with the frost fairies. The corpse had been frozen solid.

The fairies danced, their cloaks and hair lifting on the wind. The fairy holding Perriel's hand lifted one foot. Perriel smiled, stiffly, and followed the fairy into the dance, moving with the clumsiness of deep chill. Nonetheless, the graceful fairies let her join hands with them.

Gareth's hand tightened on the flap. The dance flitted before the tent, Perriel being drawn now closer, as if they taunted her with the nearness of safety (though she showed no sign of awareness), now further away.

A stride from the tent, a frost fairy released Perriel's hand. Perriel turned to the next. Gareth jumped from the tent and snagged her around the waist. She jumped, startled, but did not fight—she showed no signs of recognition, any more than she had for the tent. His mouth set, Gareth hauled her back. The snow and wind swirled faster as the fairies turned their attention on him, and icy pellets stung his face. The nearest frost fairy took a step toward him, but Gareth felt the dead air, where the tent cut off the wind, and hauled Perriel within.

A piercing wail rose from the frost fairies. He shivered, wishing he had fastened his coat before the rescue, but Perriel did not shiver. Her body had given up on warmth. His panic deepening, Gareth pulled the tent door shut and pulled off his coat. The air, chilly even inside, struck at him, but that he had to endure.

"Take your clothing off," he told Perriel. "It's not keeping you warm."

She blinked, looked down, and tugged at her coat, but the lacings slipped through her fingers. With an oath, Gareth crossed the tent. Perriel blinked occasionally as he stripped her down her shift. Damn Zavrien anyway, Gareth thought. I will not surrender her to him this easily.

"Oh, join us!" called a sweet and lovely voice from outside. Gareth's mouth set. I should have warned her before, he thought; we lost men to frost fairies every year—even men who were not cursed.

Pulling off Perriel's gloves showed that her fingers, though red with cold, were not frost-bitten. He pulled them into his hands; they felt like ice. The tent grew colder by the moment as the frost fairies lingered about it.

"Sit on my bed," Gareth said. Perriel glanced between the cots, as if trying to realize which one was which, but obeyed without being told. He pulled her boots off and pushed her under the blankets, which, fortunately, still held warmth from his body. Her eyes closed. The frost fairies' voices faded, but the tent grew colder. Gareth stripped his own clothing off, down his shirt. Without a fire, he had only one way to warm Perriel.

She barely stirred as he slid into the bed beside her and pulled the blankets over their heads. Her feet and hands, against him, were like chunks of ice. Gareth scowled. Most victims of Winter's Curse died because of monsters. He pulled her hands against his chest, and Perriel cried out in pain as warmth stripped away numbness. She started to shiver, and Gareth breathed a sigh of relief. After a moment, he reached out to grabbed their coats, and add them to the blankets about them.

Long hours later, with Perriel warm and asleep, Gareth brooded. General Ryna should not have to abandoned anyone whom she could protect to the tender mercies of Zavrien's curse. His hand traced his cheek again. If Perriel had insisted—she was only one woman, wizard or not, and could still have been forced away. By the other wizards, if need be. If they could not stand up to this Perriel, who had not even finished her apprenticeship, what good could they be against Zavrien?

Perriel's magefire burned in the tent, radiating heat without light. The midnight outside left the tent like pitch. Gareth stared across the room to Perriel's cot anyway.

"We have supplies to reach the Spell-Breaker," said Perriel, swathed in blankets. "A powerful wizard. He lives not that far outside Zavrien's lands."

"No wizard of the army ever lifted Zavrien's curse," said Gareth. "How could a wizard who never fought him?"

Perriel's blankets shifted. "Most powerful wizards aren't for hire. They don't go in for diabolerie, either, so the army does not fight them. They consider it. . . cheating."

Gareth snorted. Of all the things he might call dealing with devils, "cheating" was the last. "That's all they think of it?"

"The Art," said Perriel lightly, "is a life-long study. Not a hobby or a jest. The more powerful a wizard is, the more he has studied. A wizard interested in other things will never be as powerful as one who is not. The army, diabolerie—they are other things." She shifted again, her blankets rustling. "Every Epiphany, the priest would mention in his sermon that doubtlessly other wise men— other magi—had seen the star, but only Casper, Melchior, and Balthazar thought it worth leaving their studies for."

Gareth stared up, as if he could see the canvas overhead.

"There are wizards," said Perriel, more dryly, "who have let Zavrien's lands swamp them. Whose studies have continued unabated, when surrounded by snow."

Gareth looked through the dark with narrowed eyes. She had undercut her own point. "Wouldn't they find lifting the curse something—different?"

"The Spell-Breaker studies the breaking of spells—and the Winter's Curse would be a new spell for him." Gareth heard little conviction in her voice. Then she lowered her voice. "We can't stay here. The frost fairies know where we are."

She was right there.

Gareth thought of letting the creatures kill them—and revolted. One thing to suffer under a curse, and another to grovel before it.

General Dirk had killed himself rather than bring the curse on the army, he remembered. He turned his face into his pillow, as if he could hide from that memory.

Perriel's voice drifted across the tent. "They use our spells for the maps, to determine distance and direction. And I have a map. I can see that we do not go in circles."

He could kill himself getting her out of Zavrien's lands. Perhaps *she* could escape.

Clouds of charcoal gray billowed in the west; it was evening, but light vanished more swiftly than that alone would bring. They needed to find shelter, Perriel knew, but when they should trudge onward, she could not stop looking about at things that would never provide enough. Ragged tree trunks, torn to shreds, with snow and ice caught in the gaps. Chunks of wood sprawled, here and there breaking through the snow, as if some giant smashed the trees—which, she supposed, was possible.

"They exploded," said Gareth.

"What?"

"The trees froze and exploded," said Gareth. "I've gathered firewood from forests like this. And we—" His face was grim. Suddenly, he no longer seemed her own age. "The armies avoid forests, for fear Zavrien will attack with like cold."

He walked on, and she, still considering, scrambled alongside him. "That means—that means we can take no shelter from intact trees—that was why we, the army, did not camp near the firs—"

His mouth twitched. "*We* can take shelter by them. The army could not, but—" He pointed at his cheek. "Zavrien does not plague the cursed with more magic. He lets the curse take its course."

Her mouth pursed. "What if new spells are not needed? It is winter, it grows cold—"

He shook his head. "His spells cause the winter, it does not act naturally and turn bitter cold on occasion." He glanced at her. "And the frost fairies can't make it that cold, either."

For small blessings, give thanks—perhaps when they found a grove that could still shelter two wanderers. These could not.

Past the ruined trees, he picked out a hill. "We'll camp here."

She hurried to help him with the tent. The storm moved quickly; before they were done, it began to rain. Gareth scowled. "Worse than snow. Get inside."

Perriel looked at him in surprise, even as she obeyed.

He followed her in. "It will freeze. And then it will be ice all over."

Perriel remembered the few patches she had slipped on, hidden here and there. If everywhere was ice. . . . Her mouth shut.

"You'll have to warm the tent, so that it does not ice over," said Gareth. "Too much snow will fall off when it rises too high. Too much ice will cling, and grow heavy, and then—" He spread his hands.

She cast the spell.

The cloudless sky was brilliant and intensely blue. The oaks glittered like diamonds from the ice that encased their branches. A breeze sent dazzling chips of ice, and branches entombed in them, splattering. Gareth shifted his pack. The ice storm had covered the snow with a crust, but every step broke through with a crunch. It could be much worse—even if he and Perriel had both fallen more than once.

"We can camp again if you're tired," Perriel said. White clouds puffed from her mouth with her words. "Better than letting you sicken again." She gestured to a grove ahead, dark even in the snow. "The firs would give us some shelter."

Perriel, perhaps, was not used to the marches. He nodded. Whatever she dreamed of wizards and help against the curse, it wasn't as if they had to go somewhere. She hiked up the straps of her pack on her shoulders and plodded on.

Beneath the firs, the snow sank to a blanket on the ground, peppered with golden fir needles. The trees cut off a wind Gareth had not been conscious of.

A cluster of rocks stuck through the snow and fir needles. Perriel stared.

"What is it?" Gareth asked.

Perriel's hand pointed the line that the rocks ran in, no higher than her knee in any place, with loose stone to either side. "Stone wall. Probably from a farm. This was all farmland once."

Gareth gave her a sideways look and spoke coolly. "There are stone walls about here. We've seen a number over the years." Often with skeletons huddled in the lee. "Not collapsed piles of rocks."

Her hand swept the air. "Those were farms when Zavrien struck. This—must have been abandoned before then. Years before. But—" She scowled as if looking at something. "If I remember the map right, these hills were not good for farming.

Many farmers abandoned them after roads improved, and more food could be brought in."

He did not dispute it. Walls, in his experience, meant there might be shelter nearby and not much else.

Perriel blinked. "Haven't you heard the story? I thought that most of the soldiers had fought Zavrien for as long as they had been in the army."

Gareth's mouth set. He would not admit that it had never occurred to him that there was much of a story. Zavrien was there, and they fought him.

"Of course," Perriel said, reflectively, "I heard the story in my apprenticeship, and not since I joined the army. I doubt it would help fight him."

Gareth felt a snap of resentment. It was not his fault that he was no wizard. But Perriel was looking about.

"Let's find the farmhouse—that'll be better shelter—and I'll tell you."

Gareth choked his temper down. It was not Perriel's fault, either. And if they quarreled, she had nowhere to go.

Perriel stepped over the ruined wall and walked out from teh firs. "Once upon a time, there was a city here—I forget its name. You would never have seen it, or its ruins. They're the center of Zavrien's lands, the very heart, and his stronghold. But it was a thriving city, surrounded by farmlands, filled with merchants, with many wizards."

Another line of scattered stone broke through the snow. Perriel stepped over it.

"Zavrien was a wizard and a lord in it. Some other lord used an arcane law to cheat Zavrien, and Zavrien conjured an imp to plague the other lord—just an imp, not some great fiend."

The wind came over the field, and snow hissed before it. Perriel pulled her coat more tightly about herself. "In that hollow, there?"

Gareth grunted with surprise. A chimney stood, with three walls about it and a half-intact roof. "Better shelter than we've had for a while." They plugged through the snow.

Perriel went on as if she had not broken into her own story. "The other lord found out who had conjured the imp. Zavrien summoned a demon to protect himself from justice. The demon taught him to summon up a storm that would ward them off." Her mouth quirked. "The storm went further than Zavrien intended. No one for many miles around survived, except Zavrien himself."

Gareth remembered skeletons, littered about: grown men and women, children, little babies.

She reached the opening in the farmhouse. "Ever since then, he's lived in the ruins and conjured up spirits to do his work, and to protect him from paying for what he did."

"And add to what he will pay if he ever must," said Gareth, dryly.

"Oh, yes," said Perriel. "The land under snow's grown because it's safer that way."

She plunged into the house. Gareth followed. A thin layer of snow—even thinner than under the firs—covered the dirt floor. With a sigh of relief, he let his pack slide off.

Perriel unslung her own and worked her fingers as if they were stiff. After a minute, she moved them in familiar gestures: the magefire. Blue light popped into the air over Perriel's hands, flickering with aquamarine and violet. The fire cast multi-colored shadows across her face.

She grinned at his intent gaze. Gareth blushed and looked away; though this was the first time she had caught him, he had stared every time.

"Like magic?" said Perriel.

"Yes," said Gareth, trying to keep his longing from his voice. He stepped closer to warm his hands.

"Parents couldn't afford an apprenticeship?"

Gareth said, "I was an infant oblate."

Perriel's thoughts warred in her face: what to say in consolation—if anything could console. Gareth looked away. Many parents who offered their children were too poor to feed them. Others offered their children to atone for their sins or to keep the children from impeding the sins. His shoulders hunched. The army ought not to take such children, but how could they refuse any help with the wizards? Even with all the infant oblates, the army never had enough men.

"Did—do you know what kind of wizard you wanted to become?" Perriel said, with determined cheerfulness.

Gareth blinked. He had tried to not even think of it; few soldiers even of those who showed promise were sent off to learn magic. "Wizards are wizards, aren't they?"

"Oh, no," Perriel said. "Some master spells of knowledge, some of form and motion, some of weather. . . ."

"Like Zavrien?"

"Not before the demon taught him," said Perriel. "Perhaps that's why he didn't know how strong it was—some of disenchantment, some of illusion."

As he had had any chance to become any kind of wizard. "No, I did not know."

Silence fell for a minute.

"I could teach you a spell or two," Perriel said. "It might prove useful."

Ever hopeful Perriel. Gareth pointed at his cheek. "It would go awry—somehow—and likely kill us."

Perriel's eyebrows went up. "If our plight is that desperate, it would be quicker and cleaner than many other ways to die."

Gareth looked away. She still did not realize how dire their plight was.

Perriel sighed. She crouched to open her pack. "I wonder how the army fares."

"Not well," snarled a voice behind them. Perriel whirled. Gareth looked up. Brand, his expression fierce, glared at him as if Gareth were a wild animal and not, only weeks ago, his comrade-in-arms. His face was caked with blood; his clothing was grimy, tattered, and blood-stained. Gareth took a step forward.

"I saw the light, I should have known it would have to be you two monsters. . . ." Brand's chapped lips pulled back from his teeth. "You should know, Gareth. General Dirk knew what to do. You had his example, but you brought your curse on us."

Perriel gestured aimlessly, her voice protesting and light. Her gaze went between them. "He was unconscious; Corry and I brought him. . . ."

Brand's smile grew more feral. "That fool Corry should have known—Winter's Curse. . . the first to fall." Perriel gasped. "But not the last." He leaned forward, toward her, his voice deepening. "And you brought this on us. General Ryna was right to leave you; it's not *his* fault, but *yours*."

Perriel, deathly pale, stepped backwards. "Hold him off!"

Brand snarled and lunged, knocking Gareth sprawling. The ground hit like another blow, and Gareth fought for breath. Perriel stood somewhere behind him; he had to buy her time. Brand loomed over him. Gareth kicked, unbalancing him, and scrambled up in the brief respite.

"You wretched. . . ." Brand's words froze in mid-sentence, his face as contorted and immobile as a gargoyle's.

Moments inched by. Finally, Gareth turned.

Perriel, breathing hard, lowered her hands and spoke, very lightly. "That should hold him." Her voice grew even lighter. "Did you know him?"

"He was a soldier in the army, in my company. He was my friend." Gareth stepped back. At least, he had called him his friend, and now— "Is he dead?"

"I could release him." Her mouth contorted in derision. "The spell will wear off in hours." The wind whistled around the farmhouse. She shuddered. "What disaster befell the army?"

Gareth's eyes closed at the thought of marching on. "We have to leave. The only safety we could find here would be to slit Brand's throat."

Perriel shoved the magefire toward the immobile man with jerky hands. "He can not move, but he can still freeze. We have to leave this."

"It could attract—things," Gareth said. Half-described monsters flooded his thoughts.

Perriel's mouth set in unhappy lines. "It attracted him—but we can hope that the spell wears off first. The one mercy of this winter is that there are few wild beasts about." She slung on her own pack, her movements convulsive.

Gareth reached for his pack. "Who was Corry?"

Her voice was light and distant. "We were neighbors as children, and our parents apprenticed us to the same wizard. When the wizard. . . died before our apprenticeship was done, we took service with the army together."

And now, thought Gareth, he was dead. Her eyes were suspiciously bright, but she was not actually weeping.

"They must have been attacked not long after they left us." The words plopped out, without significance. "Not a day or two, or the morning we marched out, but we did not rest that long. For him to catch up to us, they had to have—" He shook his head.

She flinched and glanced sideways at him. "Was he tracking us?"

"The soldiers who survived must have scattered over the landscape. One was bound to happen on us." If there were enough alive to spread that far. He wondered how many men he had known had survived. Perhaps none beside Brand. He shuddered. He knew that his eyes, unlike Perriel's, were dry.

Perriel straightened her pack and spoke woodenly. "We have to find a wizard who can lift the curse."

As the farm vanished behind them, Perriel said, "Who was General Dirk?"

"He was the third or fourth to fall under the curse. He killed himself."

"That would be a sin," Perriel said. Despite her efforts, her voice was thin. Gareth looked away. She scowled, studying his face. Then, she snapped, "Don't even think it," and managed to put some strength into *that*.

Gareth blinked.

"Abandon me in the middle of the howling wilderness? Under a curse? Promise me that."

Gareth's voice was lifeless. "Some of Dirk's companions when he was cursed survived."

"You've seen how helpless I am among the snows." She drew a deep breath. "I never faced blizzards before this campaign. I would have died among the frost fairies. . . ."

Gareth's face was unmoved.

"You can not mean to abandon me!" She felt the tears starting to her eyes. She was panicking herself, she realized, but she did not even try to blink them away. Shameless, shameless, she told herself.

Gareth looked away. "I promise," he whispered.

She let her breath out slowly. It would, she told herself virtuously, help keep him alive as well.

Two days later, they sat beneath a cliff-face, contemplating the prospect of snowfall. Gareth eyed the clouds. Though they were no more than ash gray, he declared, "No farther."

It was not yet noon. Perriel did not argue. She eyed the clouds, hoping it would reveal whatever differences Gareth had seen, but then turned aside. The cliff would shelter them as long as the wind did not turn.

She glanced at Gareth. "I could show you the magefire. It would help pass the time."

His glance was sidelong. "I could burn down the tent."

"We will set the tent up and put my magefire inside it, to warm it. Then do it a few strides away. That way, we will not go crazy from boredom. We could sit about for *hours*." She smiled, mischievously. "That was how I wandered into the frost fairies' reach; I was bored."

Gareth glowered, but said, "It'll pass the time, I suppose." He slung his pack along the stone and reached for the tent.

Perriel reached for the canvas. Theory before practice would sort out whether Gareth truly wanted to be a wizard. "Actually, we do not *make* the magefire. A wizard can not *make* anything. He can only transform or transport."

"And which is magefire?" said Gareth, his voice sullen.

"Transport," said Perriel. "You snatch some sunlight from the sky and pop it through a hole."

Gareth scowled in thought.

"My old master used to say that a wizard who claimed to *make* anything was a diabolist," said Perriel. "Because he was lying, and the Devil is the father of lies." Her old master. Her lightness slid away. She wondered if she should have told Gareth that Master Rodger had been executed for diabolerie, and that she and Corry had turned him in. Corry. She swallowed. If he had not feared being abandoned by the army—why, Corry might be alive to that day.

Perriel sniffed. She could *not* teach Gareth while wailing. And if she had nothing to do, she would dwell on Corry's death until she went insane.

Gareth studied her. When she tugged on the canvas, he moved to raise it. Minutes later, Perriel stood in the tent and summoned up the magefire—the dark magefire, which brought only heat and no light, and could attract neither monsters nor soldiers. That done, she turned to Gareth. "Let's go."

Gareth raised an eyebrow, but followed her out into the snowfall.

"What you need to conjure up is a hole between here and the sky."

Gareth glanced up. Snow started to drift toward the ground.

"Past the clouds," she said, as snow clung to her arms. "The sun never stops shining up there. Not even at night—you must just pick the right portion of the sky." Laboriously, she went through the incantation and gesture. It was the first spell a wizard learned, which meant she had learned it long ago herself. The snowfall had thickened before she was done.

"Now, try it." Her heart beat faster. Wizards taught this as the first spell because failure seldom proved dangerous, but Gareth did lie under Winter's Curse. . . .

He lifted his hands. She did not dare say anything before him, or even step back, to perturb his confidence. The incantation came sharply through his teeth, and a dot of red and orange, like a coal from the center of the fire, or a fire opal from a dragon's hoard, hung in midair. It gleamed, brilliantly.

Gareth's jaw dropped.

The light vanished, but he did not stop staring until his gaze went down to his hands.

Perriel smiled. Her own first one had not lasted much longer.

"The rest," she said, "is practice."

Gareth slowly turned his head to look at her. Her smile broadened. He smiled back and looked, for a moment, younger than she was. A foolish thought considered that Gareth was more handsome than Corry, or many men in the army, or living by her old master's. She strangled it—lust had no place when they wrestled with curses and death—and the snow fell more thickly even over the last few moments.

"Try it again," she said. "It won't strain you for some time. And it would be be wise to have it ready."

A week later, the noon sky was the purest of blue, and the light glancing from the snow, almost painfully bright, but a gust hit them with powdery snow as they hurried behind a hillside.

Perriel slapped her hands against her legs to knock the snow off. "I think we're nearing the borders of Zavrien's lands."

"We'd need more luck for that than I expect."

The curse, thought Perriel, does not make him make these delightful retorts. His practice with the magefire, all week, had given him more skill than she had had after studying that long. Last night he had even warmed their tent, alone, without disaster.

Gareth looked over the snow ahead, his gaze traveling to two hillocks ahead. "Soldiers from the army," he said, his voice low, pointing at the blood-stained and ragged group.

Her anger sank to forlornness. Even she could see at a glance that no one had seen them yet, but they could not stay even in the shelter of the hillside. They moved back into the wind. Gareth looked as grim as death. Perriel's head bowed. She trudged on, staring at the blank whiteness before her feet. They might never reach the Spell-Breaker, however easily she had urged the path on Gareth.

They climbed a hill, and she carefully heeded Gareth's directions, before the soldiers could see them against the sky. And then they slogged onward. Their shadows lengthened on the snow before them.

She slowly summoned up Master Rodger's lessons. She had first thought of the Spell-Breaker because of the aptness of his skill, but the age had other wizards of great power. She had known—she had told Gareth—that some wizards lived in Zavrien's lands... she laid her knowledge against their path.

"There's a wizard," she said slowly, "who lives near here, called the Wizard of the Golden Tower." No excitement in her voice, she noted. "She is very powerful—and the Golden Tower's closer than the Spell-Breaker." She turned her face toward him. "It's in Zavrien's lands."

"You," said Gareth dryly, "are the one who knows anything about wizards."

She stopped in her tracks to look at him. He raised an eyebrow. After a minute, she told him how they had to change their path.

"And you're doing well enough with the magefire," she added. "This evening, I start to teach you the map spells."

"Will we have time to learn them before the tower?" said Gareth dryly.

"You know how storms can blow up without warning. And how deep the snow can get, to slow us even in fair weather."

The evening sky gleamed pink and yellow over the mountains. Gareth inspected the landscape for shelter. Perriel's head was bowed, her blond hair straying from her braids to loop over her cheeks. His mouth tightened; she never admitted to exhaustion. Even though there was no point in her pressing herself in the foolish hope that this wizard of the Golden Tower would manage what generations of army wizards had failed in.

"We had best camp soon," he said. "Find shelter before the light fails."

"We could find the Golden Tower before nightfall," said Perriel, though her voice held little hope. He looked out over the slopes. Snow, snow, snow—here a tree, there a cliff-face—no sign of habitation—but much that could hide a building, even a tower.

"How far?" He had yet to fully master the mapping spells, he had to rely on her—and her sunny hope of finding it easily.

"I think. . . ." said Perriel, straightening. Then she hurried forward, her gaze on a slope ahead. He followed, and she turned to him and pointed.

A golden orange tower perched on the mountain side, over a frozen lake. One pitch black window looked down on them, just visible at this distance. Loose gray shale surrounded it, the flat stones ready to fall at a touch.

His eyes narrowed. He could not make out a door, and—. "No road to it," he said dourly.

Perriel laughed, as merrily as birdsong in spring. "A wizard powerful enough to raise the curse needs no road." And then she ran off, her braids and loose hairs flying behind her.

Wizards, Gareth thought. Half-formed thoughts of what protective enchantments the wizard could have waiting for them drifted through his mind—the monsters distorted by his ignorance. He sighed. With the curse, something had to lurk in their path, but she would never believe him.

"Gareth!" Perriel stood half way up the slope, her hands on her hips. Gareth climbed after. He bent his head to watch his footing; the ultimate in irony would be for the curse to break their ankles at the doorstep of a wizard who could help them.

A choked cry came from ahead of him. A glow of gold surrounded Perriel, freezing her in mid-stride. His foot landed on an unsteady slab, and he barely kept to his feet, but he could not look away. He should never have let her get so far ahead.

The gold shimmered. Gareth tried to jump to her aid, taking no heed for his footing. His feet slid out from under him, and gold suffused his vision, all but blinding him. But he did not fall to the stones he could barely see below him. He could not even hear himself breathing.

Gloom surrounded him, and he fell again. He threw his hands out and caught himself on a flagstone floor. The dark gray slabs were cold and rough against his hands, and something scrabbled on the stone beside him. With a grunt, he pushed himself up. Perriel, her feet braced, already stood beside him, staring ahead at the walls; her face was white. Gareth dragged in a deep breath. The still air felt warmer than outside. Perhaps it was warmer.

A door, beside them, opened on a stairway. A single window looked white by contrast to the walls and floor. Gareth pushed his hood back. In the center stood a table, thick as a butcher's board and of dark brown oak. Past it, the cabinets glinted with glass or metal, and on an abundance of shelves, books overflowed.

A wizard stood behind the table. Dove gray robes swathed her to the floor, making her almost invisible among the shadows. There might be silvery runes on the robes; he could not be sure. Her hood hid the face behind, but Gareth could feel the eyes watching him.

Her voice was colder than the winter. "What brings two from the army to the door I do not have?"

Perriel flinched.

The wizard's voice rolled on. "The captains of that army know that I have no door to my tower. And why I do not. Why did they not warn you?"

"The army did not send us," said Gareth. He swallowed, trying to clear the hoarseness from his words. "The army wants nothing to do with us. We came seeking aid to lift a curse."

He could hear his heart hammer in the silence. Perriel had managed to give him some of her hope. But to reach that hope, he would have to show her what he wanted. He turned his head, revealing the mark.

Silence fell. He swallowed. She could cast them out as easily as she brought them in, and they could break their necks in the fall if she did. Powerful though she was, she might be wiser if she did, leaving them alone to suffer the curse.

"I have heard of Winter's Curse before," the wizard murmured, "but never seen it."

Perriel bit her lip. Gareth swallowed again. She had not said that she had no interest in such matters.

"Interesting." The wizard spread the word over several moments. Her voice sounded almost faraway, and her eyes unfocused. "Zavrien has wrought this spell with all his power—and disguised it well. I will need days to unravel it."

Gareth's heart slowed like a racer reaching the finish line.

The wizard tilted her head. "Have you eaten, lately?"

"We have supplies," Perriel said, weakly.

The wizard pointed at the door, though her hand was still invisible beneath the gray cloth. "The kitchen is at the bottom of the stairs. I must prepare."

Perriel scurried. Gareth followed her, to stairs even more gloomy than the room. He thought of magefire, considered the wizard upstairs, and decided the stairs were well-lit enough.

Here and there, as they descended, doors stood—solid oak, bound with dark metal—but Gareth did not even wonder what lay behind them. They had no locks, he noted, with a bit of amusement.

Halfway down, a window's glow lightened the stairway. "I wonder," said Perriel, "if she knows what she looks like."

Gareth blinked. "How could she?"

"Wizards can forget everything. My old master. . . ." Perriel hesitated. "Corry and I had to roust him out of his books for our lessons."

"Admirable lack of vanity if so," he said, dryly.

The stairs looped around the tower twice. Their footsteps resounded, and then the kitchen opened out. Cabinets stood to one side. Its hearth was big enough to hold an ox, but cold. Though soot marked the stones, no firewood stood beside it, and no ash within it. The only light came from a window that opened to the slate-covered hillside. Perriel looked out and said, "Door or no door, we could have climbed through that."

Gareth went past the table and stools to the cabinets. Unlike the other furniture in the kitchen, the cabinets were adorned: fruit and wheatears carved in the wood. Fresh, ripe food. Even with the little he knew about wizards, that looked promising. As long as the food needed no cooking.

"That route, the wizard might not have approved of," he said. "She might even have kicked us out without a meal."

He pulled the cabinet door open. It moved stiffly, if silently, and behind it, the shelves were almost empty. His eyebrows went up. Perhaps wizards were less concerned about the flesh, but then—would she not have enchanted it to fill up, so she did not have to concern herself?

He crouched to survey all the shelves. Some dried-out fruit, and an ancient loaf of bread, sat on the lowest shelf.

"What have we got?" said Perriel, turning from the window, and her gaze fell on the cabinet. For a moment, she did not seem even to breathe. Then she strode over, half-closed the doors to study the carvings, and yanked them open. Her breath came so lightly and so quickly that he swallowed. She must have recognized the cabinet, and she had not expected this.

Perriel poked the bread, and it crumbled into dust. Her expression went through several variants of disbelief. She touched the fruit, gently, with her finger; then she jabbed it. It did not crumble—or move.

After a moment, she swept away the remnants of the bread. She eyed the shelf as if expecting nothing to happen—as if she checked that another loaf would not appear.

"That wizard can't eat here," said Gareth. "No one could."

"She can not eat here." Perriel's voice sounded as remote as a frost fairy's, and she had turned as pale as one. She turned to face him. "I told you that wizards can forget everything in their studies."

"She can't forget to eat!" Then, more weakly, he added, "She'd die."

Perriel looked back at the cabinet. "Wizards deep in study can ignore *everything* else."

"They can't ignore...."

His throat choked on the word. He could not say that they could not ignore death—and he did not need to. Perriel would assure him that they could.

He could not speak. It was hard to breathe.

And the wizard had even offered to help them!

"Are we in danger?" he said.

Her voice was clipped, precise, as if she recited a lesson. She did not glance away from the cabinet. "Whatever its intentions toward us, a ghost is dangerous to all life. To have broken the spell on this—" She tapped the cabinet. "—required a great deal of death. The stone outside may not be Zavrien's work. She might have blighted the grass from the ground." Her gaze darted toward the window. "I helped once, restore land a ghost had blighted. As a prentice, but it took many spells."

She turned to face him. "If we stay here, she will sap the life out of us." Her voice lowered. "She seems fascinated enough with the curse that she would not let us leave."

Interest, thought Gareth bitterly.

"We could try to escape." Perriel bit her lower lip. "If she tries to stop us—it might not be too difficult to stop her. Her ghostly life comes from her not having noticed. We would have to make her notice." She drew in a deep breath and let it out again. "It takes time for a ghost to fade. The more she sees that proves it, the swifter it will happen. But even as a ghost fades, it can cast spells."

Gareth felt his face set into a bitter mask. He had let Perriel convince him that the curse might be broken. He should have known better.

"We can see if we can get out the window," said Perriel. She started to turn toward it.

The wizard's voice echoed in the stairway. "Have you eaten?"

Before Perriel could move, the wizard finished descending. Her feet touching the stone made no sound. How could they—how could *she*—have missed that, when their footsteps had clattered and resounded? Gareth swallowed. He was not even certain that she cast a shadow.

Then the wizard stood in the kitchen. "Have you?"

"No," said Perriel, stepping from the cabinet. Gareth pulled back, unwilling to even stand close as the wizard glided across the floor, though the air did not feel cold, or dry, or dead, from her passing. He swallowed again. Was she walking? Or did she think of moving, without noticing that she had no legs?

"Was something wrong?" the wizard said, drifting toward them. "I have always found the food sustaining."

"When you ate," Perriel said, heavily.

The wizard looked at her sleeves and raised her hands. The sleeves fell back from the wizard's hands: graceful, strong, bone-white—translucent.

Gareth retreated, aware that soon his back would reach the wall. His foot scrapped on the stone.

The wizard raised her head at the noise. The hood fell back from the face of a middle-aged woman, her expression contorted with fury into inhuman lines. "Why did you come to plague me? I curse you! I curse you!" Her voice grew less human with every word, taking on harshness like a crow's. "I curse you! May your path be forever a maze to you! May...."

Gareth lunged at her. His arms went through cloth and body as if nothing was there. He staggered through a patch of icy air, colder than he had ever faced in Zavrien's lands, and his blood felt congealed in his veins. He collapsed against the wall, his hand taking his weight.

The wizard looked over her shoulder. Her face was a shadow on the air; it contorted with hatred and was gone.

"That," said Perriel, her voice a croak, "was wise. It proved to her that she no longer lived." Almost as pale as the wizard, Perriel hugged herself.

He felt as if he would never be warm again. "Did she. . ." Gareth picked his words with care. "Did she curse us?"

"Oh yes." Her arms tightened, spasmodically. "A curse of bewilderment. On the principles of the mapping spells, at that. I could lay it myself, though hers is stronger. Wherever place we try to go, we will not get there." After a moment, she added, "Much stronger. I have no hopes of breaking it."

I should have left Perriel, Gareth thought. No promise could justify dragging her into this. The thought weighed on his soul like lead. "It's all over, then."

"Probably." Her voice was light, flat, matter of fact. She did not look at him.

He could not explain the weight her words added to his heart.

She glanced at where the ghost had dissolved. "On the other hand," she said, her voice desperately cheerful, "we have the wizard's books. I can read them. So can you—I heard the army teaches the infant oblates to read. . . ."

"I won't know what to look for."

"Spell-breaking," said Perriel. "Anything and everything about breaking spells. Then I can see if it's useful."

"You are the wizard. The army found you master enough of spells to hire you. I—"

Perriel laughed, harshly. "Because of my mastery of spells of motion." She gestured at the cabinet. The door slammed shut, sending a gust across the room. "Not bewilderment. Not weather magic. Not disenchanting. Certainly not curses. No wizard knows everything—and if I tried too hard, I could have turned out like *her*." Her mouth set. "Not that I had much chance, after my master— died."

Gareth looked at her with narrowed eyes.

Perriel said, her voice brittle, "He was a diabolist. One day Cory and I came early for our lessons and caught him at it. We denounced him before he could do something like *that*." She gestured at the snow outside. "They executed him, but no wizard would take us as prentices, so we had to let the army hire us."

After a silent minute, Gareth said, "Your parents?"

"After they had already paid my prentice fee?" Perriel snorted. "I could support myself; they would not pay twice."

Her shoulders hunched as she looked away. She did not even glance at the stairs, and Gareth had never seen her look so defeated. He scrambled for anything to say.

"If she had no food here—do we have enough supplies?"

Perriel frowned in thought. "If this *did* work. . . ." She walked over to the cabinet. "I could not make it, but perhaps I could restore it. She might have had spells that would warm the tower as well, and fetch water." Her face lit up with a smile. "Then we could hunt long and long for spell-breaking. You might even learn to cast the spell yourself."

If I didn't bring the tower down on us, thought Gareth, but his relief at her good cheer kept the words behind his mouth. Perriel was not herself when she did not think they would survive.

She dropped her pack on the table. "Not so hungry that I want to eat our supplies early, and I do not want to drag it up and down the stairs."

Gareth thought of trekking those stairs every time they wanted to eat. "We could leave the food upstairs, and eat without leaving the books."

"Crumbs attract mice."

Gareth glanced at the waste outside. After a moment, a pink-cheeked Perriel said, "We might spill things on the books—and it's a *bad habit*. You don't want to get into bad habits."

As if they were likely to suffer from their accumulation!

"Besides, you want to move after you have read for a long time. You get stiff—and it is a harbinger of worse things." She scowled at the floor. "We should sleep down here, too."

The worse things would not have time to arrive, but Gareth peeled off his pack. She might be right about stiffness. And Perriel started back up the stairs.

She stopped at the first door. "If she had studied breaking spells and lost interest, she might have stored. . . ."

She shoved on the door. It slid open without a sound, though the cold air smelled musty. A pleasant room, beneath the dust, spread before them: wardrobe in one corner, a fireplace in one wall, a great bed opposite it. Perriel studied it intently.

Gareth scowled. "Something is wrong here."

"You remembered how tight the stairway was," Perriel said. "This room is too large. It would not fit in the tower."

Gareth looked uneasily at the room.

"A *very* powerful wizard indeed," said Perriel, brightly, pulling shut the door. "There is hope!"

In the kitchen, Perriel sat with a tome in her lap. The wizard's crabbed handwriting had not been easy to pick out from the rest of the works, many of which were equally hard to read, but she had found the right book. She trusted.

Gareth stood by the stairway—a dark, silent, *watching* shadow. She considered the cabinet again. Fruit and bread would prove a meager diet, but she did not want to try generating food that the wizard had not done before. Not when Gareth would take anything going wrong as proof of the curse's dreadful power.

"I thought wizards could not create anything," said Gareth.

"We don't," said Perriel.

"So this steals?"

He *had* listened.

"No. It *transforms*. An apple tree can make more apples from sunlight, earth, air, and water. This can do the same."

"All these spells work like that?" said Gareth. "None of them steal?"

"No," said Perriel more sharply, "but I've read her notes." She shifted the book into better light. "And thieving cabinets draw the attention of the army. Which would distract the wizard from her work."

She read the freshening spell again. Gareth shifted his weight.

"For what I am doing—freshening the spell—only contagion effects are needed," said Perriel. "Thing that are in contact continue to affect each other after they are out of contact. I have to draw them back together. You can refresh just about any enchanted thing that way, even if you can not fathom the original spell."

Gareth looked lost in thought. Perriel smiled. She might make a wizard of him yet. She intoned the words.

Moments later, the very air felt different. She closed the book. Gareth strode past her to open the cabinets. Fruit—not dried, but fresh—sprung up on two shelves, and a third had bread. Perriel's mouth watered: peaches, grapes, plums, apples, strawberries, and still more fruit, not all of which she could identify. She grabbed a plum and bit into its tangy pulp. She licked her lips to snag the juice. The wizard had not stinted on the spell; all the stranger, that she had forgotten to eat. Unless the spell had been only practice to her.

Perriel got down to the pit. The more fool the wizard. Gareth still stared at the cabinet, until, with a scowl, he pulled open the next cabinet: dried meat, and cheese.

Perriel finally found her voice and said, "With magefire to melt the snow, we can look as long as we need to, to find some way to break these curses."

She picked a hunk of cheese up. "She must have been a ghost long and long; that was a sturdy spell and would not have broken in a month or two of her not noticing it." She bit into the cheese, far fresher than the army's, chewed, and swallowed. "We should eat well. We need to keep up our strength for the hunt through the books."

Perriel would be safe here.

She did not need winter lore to survive in the Golden Tower, and so his promise was void. She could melt snow for water, she had plentiful food, better than the army had, and the tower would shelter her from the winter.

Gareth leaned from the window. The chill of early morning made him shiver. Which was to say, she would be safe if misfortune did not plague her. If he left, Winter's Curse would wear off. It took time, but better that than rummaging through all those books that *might* have the knowledge to break the curse. Even the master wizard, with years more knowledge than Perriel, had admitted she would have to search.

Perriel had been hopeful when she declared that they could have gotten in through the window, but out was another matter. The snow was deep enough to break his fall.

He dropped his pack into the snow. He had taken all the army supplies, and as much of the food from the cabinet as he would eat before it spoiled; that would help appease Perriel. He slung his legs over the window's edge and dropped himself.

Snow sprang through every gap to worm its way under his clothing, sometimes to his bare skin. Gareth gasped. He sat up, shed as much snow as he could, and grabbed his pack. He might even seek out this Spell-Breaker that Perriel had spoken of.

First, he had to escape the Golden Tower and Perriel. He slung on the pack and eyed the landscape. The eastern sky was pale yellow with dawn. He could travel far today, and all he had to do was get away.

The wind made the snow hiss over itself, the fine grains already blurring the edges of where he fell. It would worm its way under his hood, through the lacings of his cloak.

Perriel would say that he should walk with his back to it.

Grimacing at the thought, but unable to say why, Gareth walked away.

Perriel looked up from a stack of books. Morning light spread from the window over the room, revealing row on row of books— the sun had risen high enough that it did not shine directly through the window—and no sign of Gareth. She scowled and shoved back her chair. He did not think their escape likely, but what sort of excuse was that to dawdle over a meal? She stalked down the stairs to the kitchen, where their cots stood.

The kitchen stood empty.

The window stood open a crack, and a chilly draft drifted over the floor despite the spells. Perriel, feeling as numb as if the cold had frozen her, walked over. Beneath, the wind-swept snow showed dips and rises, but no tracks.

Perriel dragged in her breath and, to be sure, climbed the stairs, testing each door and finding the dust behind untroubled, until she reached the top, without a sign of Gareth. She looked uneasily about. She was not the new wizard of the Golden Tower, she was not *that* lost in her studies, she would have heard Gareth returning.

Carefully, she looked about the room. Then she inspected each corner where Gareth might have hidden from view. Biting her lip, she crept down the stairs again: she had not ransacked the kitchens for hiding places.

She peered up the chimney, but that was clear, and then looked about. Beneath the stairway stood another door. Her heart hammered. If Gareth had noticed it, and gone in—she had not thought there might be other dangers, believing the ghost's presence would have dealt with *them* as well. But there could be dangers in a wizard's tower that did not leave.

Oddly enough, the door opened to a small corridor, leading under the stairs, as if nothing else would fit. Perriel summoned up the magefire to glow over her shoulder, and walked inside. Another room appeared before her. With tubs and screens, and pumps for water. Perriel stared at it. One thought intruded: no more need to melt snow for water. She shook her head, and another thought succeeded that one: she itched for the want of bathing, her hair was filthy, and her clothing she had worn for weeks.

If Gareth had found it, he might have washed himself, but then he would have told her.

Perriel stalked from the room. Gareth did not hide there. It was like trying to lean on a wall, only to find it a glamour, and staggering without a bit of balance.

Outside, the wind bore a veil of fine snow. How long had Gareth been gone? How hard had the wind blown? Enough to cover his tracks?

How *could* he? Perriel buried her face in her hands. He had promised—he had—but only not to abandon her in the winter wilds. She felt herself shaking and could not even try to stop it. He suffered under two curses now, and he had thought one was reason enough to give up hope.

Gareth must have thought to save her by losing himself, she realized.

She let out her breath very slowly. The dear, sweet *idiot*.

She shook her head. She must not—that would do Gareth no good, and someone had to think of his well-bring. She thought of the tracks again, and ran over the books she had been reading. One had mentioned of a far-seeing spell. It would let her find Gareth at least.

She bolted for the stairs. Ever-living and all-merciful God, let her find Gareth and save the fool from freezing to death. "Lord have mercy, Christ have mercy, Lord have mercy. St. Casper, pray for me. St. Melchior, pray for me. St. Balthazar, pray for me."

The sky was colorful again, this time with fiery red and vivid gold. His pack weighed on his shoulders; it had not felt that heavy when he and Perriel arrived at the Golden Tower. Gareth sighed. It had been a troublesome day. The baffling contortions of hills had not made it easy to find his way.

Perriel would inquire why, if it did not matter where he was going, it mattered so much if he could tell his way. He could almost see her asking it, bright-eyed and smiling.

Gareth groaned and plodded about the hill. There, on a slope covered with loose rock, stood a tower, golden in the sunset—or rather, more golden in the sunset. Gareth stopped. He could see the window. If Perriel stood at it, she could see him.

His shoulders slumped. Finally, he turned away, hoping that being this close would not affect Perriel again.

He collided with something. Nothing was there, he could see the snow before him, but he put forth his hand, and ran it over a wall, as transparent as air, and far harder to advance against than the wind.

Perriel's voice carried over the snow. "Don't even try."

He looked back. During the moment he had turned away, she had appeared in the window. Thin as it had sounded, her voice could not carry that far.

Then, she was a wizard.

She leaned out of the window, and spoke as if she stood next to him. "I won't let you. If you try, you will make me waste even more time than you already have."

Gareth's hands clenched into fists.

"*She* cursed you, too. Didn't you listen? Our journeys will be mazes; we will be unable to go where we wish—until we break that one as well. Winter's Curse takes precedence, as more dangerous."

Slowly, Gareth forced his hands to relax. He walked toward her, and Perriel, without a word, pulled back into the tower but watched his every step. At the foot of the tower, he looked at her, for some reason certain that she, and not Corry, had determined that they had to denounce their master for his diabolerie.

He felt ready to weep. All the effort had gone to nothing.

"How do you intend to get me up there?" he said.

Perriel felt light-headed. "Stand there." Her tongue touched her lip. She did not want to have the spell falter and give Gareth a moment to reconsider. She had lifted things with the shield spell before, but it was tricky, and none of them had been easy to damage, or hard to replace. And she had not had giddy thoughts haunting her with the knowledge that he was alive, he was well, he was back. . . .

She drew a deep breath before she cast it.

Gareth rose so smoothly that she had to scramble out of the way, to let him in the window. He stepped in—alive, intact, uninjured, moving without any hesitation and showing no signs of bruises, or even cold. For a moment, after shutting the window, Perriel just stood and watched him. He took off his pack and coat as easily, as well.

Gareth would have a hard time explaining why *this* was a manifestation of the curse, but she felt so gleeful that she did not point that out, only danced across the floor and yanked open the door.

"Look. Baths."

Gareth looked as if he were about to waver. Then he said, slowly, "Aren't there magical creatures that live in springs?"

"*Live*, Gareth, *live*. No matter how magical they are, the ghost's presence would have killed them years ago." She stepped inside and grinned. "There's even soap. A ghost did not affect *that*. And, of course, there's no way to heat the water because a wizard needs only magefire."

Her grin deepened. Perhaps she should see if there were any spells to conjure up clothing. Then they would have all that they needed.

His absence had done her no harm, but Perriel in her elation looked more like a princess rescued from the dragon's maw than a maiden under a deadly curse.

"Food, first," he said.

After a moment, she shrugged. "Certainly let us eat," she said, half-laughing. "A feast to celebrate the safe return of the traveler."

Her eyes were bright. Her braids had not quite kept her hair subdued; strands formed an aura about the braids, and he found himself wondering what she would look like clean, well clad, and unharried.

The sounds of water filling the tub and of cloth being shed reminded her that he was on the other side of the screen. Gareth had lit his bath with his own magefire; the red glow was invisible, except where reflected from the ceiling. She forced her gaze away.

She kept her own violet-blue light low. The water surface, choppy from the water flowing in, reflect a pattern of black and violet.

She shed her clothing, slid within, and let the warmth ease about her. She tugged at her hair, at the braid that she had done and undone, but had never properly combed out in the wilderness.

Wet and free, it swam about her like a mermaid's—though it would be like damp seaweed once she got out.

She reached for her comb. The sounds from the other side of the screen showed that Gareth was climbing into his bath. She set about applying soap and comb to her hair. He had been foolish indeed, leaving like that, but now, giddy with his safe return, she would concede that the fool had done it with the sincere desire to protect her.

She snorted. As if a maid who had denounced her own master for his diabolerie needed much in the way of protection. She swept her hair about the water to rinse it out.

Gareth must have wanted only to get away from the Golden Tower. If he tried to reach another place, such as the Spell-Breaker's lands, he would have missed it, but he might, instead of circling round, have made it to a third place. She chuckled. She would not mention that flaw to him, but that he had not noticed was enough to show that Winter's Curse was not a death sentence. They had a chance.

She reached for the soap again, and grabbed it too tightly. It leapt, slippery, from her fingers, out of the tub, and clattered on the floor. Silence came from the other side, making her keenly aware of the noises that had ended. Her mouth twisted. Nothing like clumsiness to show how competent she was to look after herself. She clambered out—and her wet foot missed the step, and slid out.

She cried out in surprise, until the flagstones knocked the breath out of her.

Gareth called, sharply, "Are you all right?"

She should speak, tell him that she was all right. . . but dragging down a breath did not give her the power of speech.

Water sloshed on the other side, his footsteps sounded on the floor, and his bare hand touched her arm.

"Are you all right?"

She felt a fool. She pushed off the stone, rising to her knees. "I just fell; I'm not hurt. Bruised, maybe."

Gareth glanced at them, and she became keenly aware of their nakedness. She glanced at him, and glanced away, but her mouth still felt bone-dry. He had, indeed, suffered no injuries from his foolish journey—at least that she could see.

He dropped to one knee beside her. Despite his folly, he was back, alive and well. Her hand went out, almost without her willing it, to brush against the warmth of his arm and be sure of it.

Even beneath her tentative fingers, she felt the muscle flex beneath the skin. Gareth leaned forward. His mouth brushed hers. Alive indeed. She leaned forward to return the kiss, and put her arms about his shoulders.

The next morning, the sky was bright and clear and blue, without a cloud to be seen anywhere over the wind-swept snow. That showed no signs of Gareth's venture.

Perriel stood in the wizard's library. Though it was midmorning, and she had seen no sign of Gareth, she felt not the slightest impulse to search for him. Her body ached, and the thought made her flush.

She had been a fool—an utter fool. Even in her relief and delight that he was alive.

Her hand went over the books again. One, strangely written, was marked Simples. Perriel opened it and flipped through the pages: simples indeed, common spells that any cunning woman might know, for burns and beestings, for fertility in man or beast, and more. "A spell for sowing seeds over land—what's wrong with doing it by hand?" Perriel muttered.

She read the next, and her finger stopped as if captured. Breathing hard, Perriel read it again. For whether a woman carried a child.

She stood by the shelf a long minute. Then she yanked the book over to the table, sat, and studied.

The spell was not difficult; it took her less time than was quite pleasant to attempt it. Her heart hammering, she cast it. A soft green glow appeared between her hands, a rounded oval. Perriel cupped it between her fingers, as if it were a fragile bird's egg that she had to protect, though the green cloud, brushing her fingers, could not be felt, only seen.

She swallowed. The shades of green shifted. Green within the light, taking shape within the heart of the glow. It shifted again.

She stared in disbelief. It was, indeed, two shapes. As if one were not enough.

Her heart threw itself against her chest in its hammering. She was a fool. Thrice a fool. Gareth had told her how dangerous the curse was, again and again. First she had ignored him, and then, in her giddiness, she had acted as if she had already broken the spell. Not remembering that it lay, lurking, ready to turn folly into disaster—into their bringing the curse on an innocent child. Or rather, children.

She wished she could weep. But her eyes felt bone dry.

"Lord, have mercy," she whispered. "Christ, have mercy. Lord, have mercy. St. Michael, Archangel, pray for us." She could not think for a moment. "Holy Innocents, pray for us."

She heard footsteps on the stairs. They were slow.

Perriel sat, her hands covering her face, when he reached the tower top. Gareth squared his shoulders. If she had known what they did, so had he. He had to own his own share of the folly.

She had, he noted, braided her hair again, severely. He stepped inside the door.

She lowered her hands, and he felt queasy. She did not look ready to rail at him, but she looked more distressed than he had believed possible.

A book lay open before her. She slammed it shut. Her cheeks colored, to an unbecoming red. "I came with child."

For a long minute, the words made no sense at all. Then Gareth looked away before she could watch his face heat. His hand clenched into a fist. He should have foreseen that. Perriel had never believed the threat of the curse, and he had. He should have known the curse would find a way to worsen their plight.

"Twins," she added.

He could imagine no words of comfort, and she looked as if saying anything would break her control.

Perriel rose. Her gaze flickered past Gareth toward the books. She walked to them, but her fingers drifted over them rather than pulling any out.

He did not much want to study himself, but however desultory their reading was, it would have more hope—such as it was—than moping about. He walked up to the books, a section far from Perriel's, but the names on the bindings signified nothing to him.

"If you dismiss a book," said Perriel, dully, without looking up, "put it aside, just as if you though I should look at it. So that we do not look at books twice."

She put a book aside, off the shelf.

His arms ached. From stretching for books, from lugging them about, from standing while hunting through them—he should have sat to read, and not stood wherever he was, but if they had any hope at all, it lay in speed. He looked up from the latest tome.

The sun was setting. Gareth blinked and looked at. Setting. And not just having turned all the sunlight golden or orange. The sun set in masses of scarlet and crimson—in clouds that had also arisen without his noticing.

He lowered the book. So this was how the wizards managed to forget all in their studies.

He walked over to the empty shelf and put a book in it. This one would be ones they had dismissed. Perriel raised her hands to gesture for the magefire, and violet-blue light filled the tower room. Gareth looked at her face for a minute, comparing to soldiers who had made forced marches. Some of it might be the color the light shed, but. . . .

Besides, Perriel had never had to endure such marches. And she was with child.

"You have eat," said Gareth. The harshness of his voice surprised him, but he could not stop. "And sleep."

"I have to find a way to break the curse," said Perriel.

"You have to consider your health," said Gareth. When she opened her mouth again, he glanced at her waist.

Perriel clapped shut both her mouth and the book. In this light, he could not be sure she blushed.

Days of searching.

It would take weeks before they could declare they had searched everything, but Gareth could see that looming ahead.

God help them both, they had to discover something to free themselves. His fingers ran over the books, and he pulled one out at random. Not one showing many signs of use. Gareth flipped it open. His gaze went over pages of prayers, and readings from scripture. No wonder the wizard had not used it much; its mere presence surprised him. He fanned several pages, wondering if it contained a prayer service for times of distress. One appeared. He tried to collect his thoughts and read, "Nothing has befallen you save what is common to man."

Gareth froze. The words echoed and re-echoed in his mind. "Save what is common to man." His thoughts ran back over the last weeks. God help me, he thought, desperately.

"Gareth?" said Perriel, with more than a touch of sharpness. Her hands were full of a book, but if he had realized the truth, that was more important.

"What happened to the wizard of the Golden Tower—that has happened to other wizards, often?" he asked.

Perriel's eyebrows shot up. After a minute, she said, "Not often, but it happens. It happened to one near my master's tower. I helped restore the lands he had blighted."

He could not find words to speak.

"I suppose it would be more likely here, where wizards did not care to flee the winter." Her mouth twisted. "We care. We are not in that danger."

Gareth shook his head, trying to clear it. The frost fairies had found Perriel in the manner they had all been warned against.

"What if there was no curse?" he said, his voice barely a croak.

Perriel opened her mouth and shut it again. Then she blinked, like an owlet in noon sunlight, and stared at him. "Everyone—*you* said it was—"

"What if Zavrien said there was, and let all our ill luck be blamed on it?"

She blinked again.

"They blamed the army's defeat on us, and Zavrien already knew where they were. He was bound to attack."

Color drained from Perriel's face. "We've had—other problems."

"Nothing that can't befall someone in the winter lands."

"That would be. . ." She picked her next word slowly. "*Fiendish.*" Her hand went to her mouth. "Most of our misery has come from the army's exiling us."

His heart hammered so loudly that he was surprised it did not echo. He forced his breath out, and his thoughts roiled.

"It can't be true. Someone would have guessed by now," he whispered. "How many soldiers has he cursed?"

"How long have they lasted after?" Perriel said. She clung to her book if it were a shield. "When the army drove them off, into Zavrien's lands?" She frowned for a moment and said, sharply. "Did they cast them out from the very beginning?"

"The army has suffered defeats at Zavrien's hands. Once he had cast his forces against them, and let them blame it on the curse, they would have a reason to believe it."

Her hand went to her waist.

"Women have come with child without a curse," Gareth said. Perriel blushed. He gentled his voice. "Misfortune happens, but once Zavrien had told us all that the curse existed, we all blamed every misfortune on it."

Gareth put the book back, with care. It could not be.

"Has he ever cursed a wizard?" said Perriel.

Gareth racked his memory. "No, he has not."

Slowly, she nodded. "A wizard could watch him cast the spell and recognize it as an illusion, not a curse. And that would explain why the illusion hid the curse so perfectly." Her breath came light and fast. "I can break illusions."

Perriel puttered around for an hour after, with glasses and powders. Sunset faded, and magefire gave their only light, instead. Silvery and ruddy dust stained her fingers, and she muttered under her breath. Gareth leaned against the wall, unable to relax. If he had guessed wrong. . . his thoughts trailed off, unable to guess about consequences. A handful of spells did not make him a wizard.

"Stand there, Gareth." Perriel pointed, and Gareth walked over. She chanted in a clear high voice—a short spell—and clapped the book shut again.

"That does that. A simple spell indeed. That it broke so easily is proof that there was nothing more behind it."

Gareth tried to look down, at his cheek. The mark had never been more than a suggestion of black in the corner of his sight. Only by straining could he see that it was gone.

"I suppose," said Perriel, dryly, "that we should tell the army the secret."

Gareth said, even more dryly, "The wizard of the Golden Tower laid another curse on us. Is that one also an illusion?"

Perriel threw one hand in the air. "So I will break that one. Food, water, shelter—books!—are all to be found here, so her curse will not kill us, but we will have to escape sometime. Or at least, we will want to."

Gareth felt a cold draft but dismissed it. He glanced at her waist. "Good. I do not think that a priest will wander this far in time."

Perriel turned pink. Gareth closed the distance between them to kiss her. She turned even more pink, and did not meet his gaze, but went on, doggedly, "The confusion spell is not the Winter's Curse—nothing more than an illusion."

"Oh," said another voice, familiar, from the hallway, "there was something more to it."

Gareth felt his blood congeal. He stepped away from Perriel. She looked at the doorway and back to Gareth. Without looking, he nodded. Then he faced Zavrien.

The wizard walked in. His black robes, embroidered with coppery runes, swirled about him. The air chilled. Gareth shivered. It was not merely terror on his part; it grew colder. He glanced through the doorway. Zavrien had brought none of his creatures with him. Then, he could dispose of a half-trained wizard, and a soldier with not a dozen spells, by himself.

"I watch that spell," said Zavrien. "No one will tell the army of their own wickedness, inspired by no more than a trick on my part."

"You inflicted this on us," said Perriel, "and you call it a *trick*!"

Zavrien's lip curled. "If the army can not realize what I did, if they are such cowards, and such knaves that they abuse me for wickedness when they treacherously abandon their own, they do not deserve to know. And you will not tell them."

"*Deserve*," said Gareth.

"I had assailed them with my loyal forces before. But when I marked one of their company, they were ready to blame him. And I never had to assail them again." Zavrien glanced between them and lifted an eyebrow. "I have only watched the spell, not you. I do not know what has befallen you; I sent nothing after you. You fathomed the spell, so you know that the army inflicted the misery. They have no right to call me wicked."

"No right?" Gareth's voice cracked.

Zavrien whirled on him. "What have I done that others have not? It was *their* treachery that sent me to that—unfortunate spell, and *they* meant to do it." His eyes were large as he stared at Gareth.

That was why he talked when he laid the curse, Gareth realized; he was trying to convince me, or himself, that it was justified.

"Since then, I have only defended myself."

Gareth remembered the skeletons in the snow and felt mute.

"Your lands have spread," spat Perriel.

"What else am I to do? Permit the army to murder me? The same army that abandoned you to your deaths?"

"Says the wizard who intends to murder us," said Gareth.

"*Intends*?" said Zavrien. "I do not *intend*. You invaded my land, and I will have my rights. That it will prevent you from talebearing is also good."

Perriel braced herself. Her voice was belligerent. "You should not have left your citadel, where you are strongest."

Zavrien raised his hand. White lightning lashed out and thundered in the tiny room. Perriel threw up both her hands, drawing the lightning into them; she caught every lash, her hands darting about like minnows in a river, but she strained to do it. Zavrien smiled, more deeply, and raised his other hand. Quickly he threw it toward Gareth. Gareth lunged forward, and into a wall of air, like the one Perriel had conjured.

Zavrien, looking smug, turned his back on him.

Gareth fought to steady his breath as Perriel caught Zavrien's lightnings. He would murder her, and the babies, and then he would dispose of the soldier, who—

Zavrien had never cursed a wizard. Gareth dragged in a deep breath. Zavrien must have ensured that he was not a wizard before sending the frost fairy and giant after him. And Zavrien had bragged of not watching them since he had laid the curse.

Which meant he did not know that Gareth *was* a wizard now.

So to speak.

Gareth sidled against the wall, to ensure that he stood behind Zavrien, where no stray glance would reveal his actions. He wished for Perriel's lightless spell, where no shadow would reveal his magefire before the heat acted, but he had no time to waste on regrets.

Narrowing his eyes, he summoned magefire, blazing ruby red, and as close to Zavrien as he could conjure it. The light flared behind Zavrien; Gareth could feel the heat through the air. He pushed it forward, against Zavrien's robes. In moments, the cloth smoldered.

Gareth's heart beat, once, twice—Zavrien cried out. As if that was an order, his robes flamed. He jerked his head around, trying to peer over his shoulder.

Perriel lifted her hands, still filled with lightnings, and hurled them back. The air crackled and gleamed, and Zavrien screamed in pain. Perriel's hand rose to conjure magefire, and Zavrien's robes exploded into fire.

Zavrien screamed, loud and piercing. He staggered, and Gareth wondered what else he could set ablaze—and he was going toward Perriel.

Perriel's hands leapt through the air. Zavrien collided with her wall of air. Snarling, he clawed the air toward Gareth, and hit his own wall of air. His mouth opened again, but no shout came out. He glared at Gareth, his eyes frothing with the same hatred as when he complained of the injustice he had suffered—and then the fire leapt, and his charred body collapsed against the wall, to slide to the floor. There it lay, and burned, until it sank to smoldering.

The air stank of its smoke.

Perriel said, her voice high and light, "I didn't think that we had a chance."

Gareth said, "May God have mercy on his soul." He could get little hope into his voice, after the hatred that had contorted Zavrien in his last moments—but the man was dead. He steadied his breath.

Perriel's hands went up in a spell. After a moment, he recognized the coffin spell, even before she had conjured up the box that took in the remains—down to the ghastly smoke. Then, they had to be rid of the body. He let his breath out slowly.

Something splashed, outside. He looked at the window. Water dripped from the roof. And then a chunk of ice and snow pulled loose and plummeted.

He pushed open the window. Even in the night, warm air blew in.

"I suppose," Perriel said, lightly, distantly, "that his spells were of the manner that work only for his lifetime."

She stared out as if seeing nothing, as if trying to drink in what had happened. Slowly, a smile crept onto her face, and broadened, brighter than the dawn. She came up beside him, and cast a magefire out the window—not so warm, but brilliantly white and gold. As far as they could see, snow melted and streamed. Already bare earth showed here and there, and the patches widened as they watched.

Long minutes later, Perriel dropped the spell. "It won't finish in a moment," she said. "We should go rest, and see what the morning brings."

Gareth nodded. "We have much to consider then."

Perriel rose before he did. For a moment, his arm thrown across his face, Gareth considered going back to sleep, but her feet padded across the floor to the window, and did not stir from it, and—who knew what lay outside?

The sky was delicate pinks and creams, and beneath, the hills showed a patchwork of brown and white—white mostly in the sheltered nooks—and streams and ponds of water.

"How good for us," said Perriel, lightly. "Life is hard enough when you do not finish your apprenticeship, and you can't join the army." She turned to face him. "I do not want to give up this tower. We can study wizardry, and no doubt we will not be alone."

Gareth let out his breath. "You said that you had to help restore the land—where the wizard had died. What with the winter, I do not think Zavrien's lands will be hale. About here, there was the ghost, as well."

Perriel nodded. "I will study how to break the other curse. You will study to restore it. I did the restoration while an apprentice." Then she smiled. "And I saw a spell to cast seed over the land. We could turn it to green easily enough."

It was still dawn, the hills dark, the clouds showing shades of dark gray. Gareth looked down at the rousing town. Perriel had insisted on landing outside it, and actually walking within, but their magical arrival had been noted—and perhaps, so had the direction they had come from.

Her fingers linked with his. The crowds gathered as they walked.

"You!" called a lanky man, his face hard. Perriel's fingers tightened on Gareth's. "You know what happened *there*!" He gestured at the hills. Where the snow had been. Where green just sprouted, here and there, and yellowy with newness.

"You must, you must," said a plump woman, breathlessly. "You came from there—"

Faces full of hope and wonder and questions turned toward them. Even the youngest among them looked worn.

Perriel let out her breath. "Zavrien is dead," she called, loudly enough to heard throughout the crowd. "His spells have broken."

Gasps of surprise surrounded them, and soon a crowd. One young woman said, "It would be *safe* to live there?"

"We're living there," said Gareth.

"You're wizards," said a small girl, and in her mouth, it sounded like an accusation.

He felt keenly aware of the book he had brought with him in case he had a moment to study: *Simples*, for its curative spells. He still studied the most basic ones, and hoped to reach those to aid a woman in childbirth in time. But he could cast spells.

"That is how we know that wizardry has made the land green and pleasant, enough for others to live there as well—"

"What are you doing *here*?" said an old woman, suspiciously.

"Marrying," said Gareth. His hand tightened on Perriel's. "Before the church door and witnesses."

Their efforts had turned the hills green, but they had not restored the woods that had grown before. Even now, the slopes showed only saplings.

The town of Golden Tower had, therefore, risen up in buildings of stone, as it grew up about the foot of the tower, as peasants and merchants and tradesmen flocked to the land. Where better than where two wizards already lived—wizards from whom spells could be purchased?

Perriel smiled wryly. She and Gareth had barely fenced off enough ground for a stairway, and a garden, before the town engulfed them. They had mastered the spells to add space within the tower; they had needed to.

Elena and Kenelm, solemn as judges, weeded their corner of the garden. The younger children, squealing with glee, ran across the grass to bounce off the spell to keep them from trampling the plots—and then ran back to bounce again.

She smiled a little. They would have to add space to the garden, too, and soon.

A voice outside carried, farther perhaps than intended: "A wizard named Perriel was with General Ryna's army, but the other wizard was Corry."

She glanced at Gareth. He must have heard; he looked up from the desk.

"Still," said another soldier, "even if not that Perriel, they could help fight diabolerie. The townsfolk speak highly of their magic."

A breeze blew in the window, rustling papers.

"We could pretend we're not here," Perriel said in a low voice.

"They'll come back," said Gareth, marking his place. "The army needs wizards. It needs them very much." His mouth twitched. "They took you and Cory on. That was not kindness for two prentices who had done their duty."

The heavy clatter of the knocker resounded. Perriel sighed and turned from the window. Adding rooms to the tower had added stairs to it as well, but it still took less time than she liked to reach the door.

The captain and soldiers bowed with overt respect, but she felt cold and still.

"Good mistress, good master, we have come to appeal for your aid. Your wizardry is needed for more than the simples you provide for this town."

Perriel swallowed.

Gareth greeted them and escorted them to the room where they talked with clients. And she could read the strain in his face as he did it, and still more when they talked of the army's need for wizards as powerful as they were.

"Such powers are needed against evil wizards," said the captain.

"And their works," said Perriel. "There are still *leagues* where the depredations of Zavrien mark the land—even with all our labors, even after his death."

One soldier shifted uneasily. "Is Zavrien dead?"

Perriel hesitated. They had told the villagers, she reminded herself.

"Why else would his enchantments have failed as they did? But if he is not dead, wizards are needed here to guard against his return."

"If his enchantments failed," said the captain, "he is too weak to be any danger anymore."

"His spells still taint the land." She added, firmly, "Our magic is needed here."

"That is work that any prentice could do," said the soldier.

"If it is so easy," said Perriel, "we would have been done by now." She smiled. "Besides, we have to look after the children."

Also by Mary Catelli

Curses And Wonders
Dragon Slayer
Eyes of the Sorceress
Fever and Snow
Mermaids' Song
Sword and Shadow
The Book of Bone
Witch-Prince Ways
Dragonfire and Time
Enchantments And Dragons
Jewel of the Tiger
Over the Sea, To Me
The Dragon's Cottage
The Maze, the Manor, and the Unicorn
The White Menagerie
A Diabolical Bargain
Madeleine and the Mists
Magic And Secrets
The Lion and the Library
The Princess Goes Into The Forest
The Wolf and the Ward
The Witch-Child and the Scarlet Fleet
Treachery And Spells
Winter's Curse
Crow Curse
Free Passage
Isabelle and the Siren
Journeys And Wizardry
Lifestone

Magic of the Lost God
Never Comment On A Likeness
One Name
The Drunken Mermaids
The Turtle in the Sea of Sand
Were I You
Where There Is Smoke